My Uncle Keith Died

My Uncle Keith Died

Written by Carol Ann Loehr
Illustrated by James Mojonnier
Discussion Guide by Julianne Cosentino

© Copyright 2006 Carol Ann Loehr.

Illustrations by James Mojonnier, www.jamesmojonnier.com
Cover design and interior layout by Grinning Moon Creative, www.grinningmoon.com
Typeset in Sabon.
All rights reserved. No part of this publication may be reproduced, stored in a retrieval system, or transmitted, in any form or by any means, electronic, mechanical, photocopying, recording, or otherwise, without the written prior permission of the author.

Note for Librarians: A cataloguing record for this book is available from Library and Archives Canada at www.collectionscanada.ca/amicus/index-e.html
ISBN 1-4251-0262-X

Printed in Victoria, BC, Canada. Printed on paper with minimum 30% recycled fibre.
Trafford's print shop runs on "green energy" from solar, wind and other environmentally-friendly power sources.

TRAFFORD PUBLISHING

Offices in Canada, USA, Ireland and UK
This book was published on-demand in cooperation with Trafford Publishing. On-demand publishing is a unique process and service of making a book available for retail sale to the public taking advantage of on-demand manufacturing and Internet marketing. On-demand publishing includes promotions, retail sales, manufacturing, order fulfilment, accounting and collecting royalties on behalf of the author.

Book sales for North America and international:
Trafford Publishing, 6E–2333 Government St.,
Victoria, BC V8T 4P4 CANADA
phone 250 383 6864 (toll-free 1 888 232 4444)
fax 250 383 6804; email to orders@trafford.com
Book sales in Europe:
Trafford Publishing (UK) Limited, 9 Park End Street, 2nd Floor
Oxford, UK OX1 1HH UNITED KINGDOM
phone 44 (0)1865 722 113 (local rate 0845 230 9601)
facsimile 44 (0)1865 722 868; info.uk@trafford.com
Order online at:
trafford.com/06-2019

10 9 8 7 6 5 4 3 2 1

For Cody

Who shared this story about his Uncle Keith. Cody wanted others to know all about his Uncle Keith, to learn about depression, and to understand why his Uncle Keith died from suicide.

My name is Cody, and I am ten years old. When I was four years old, my Uncle Keith died. Our family was very sad when Uncle Keith died.

I didn't know my Uncle Keith very well because I was still young when he died, but my mother would always tell me stories about Uncle Keith.

I think I am like my Uncle Keith in many ways. Uncle Keith was always playing jokes on others — just like me. My mother said his dark eyes would twinkle like mine do when I am thinking about getting into some mischief. I loved my Uncle Keith, and I wish he didn't die so young.

Uncle Keith loved to play sports. He was a great athlete! Uncle Keith played ice hockey, ran track and cross country, and rowed on a crew team in college. I think maybe that is why I decided to play ice hockey.

Keith's mother, my Great Aunt Carol, gave me some of Keith's hockey trophies. I keep his trophies on a shelf in my room, and now I show them to all my friends. I just won a basketball trophy, and I put it right next to Uncle Keith's trophies. Trophies are cool to have, but Uncle Keith would think it is more important to have fun and be part of a team.

Uncle Keith loved nature, and he found many activities so he could enjoy the outdoors. Probably his favorite outdoor activity was fly fishing. He loved to fish! Uncle Keith made flies that looked like bugs to fool the fish. He placed a fly on his line and cast his line into the water. He was very good at making the fake fly move so that it looked real to the fish. Since fish love to eat bugs, they jumped at the fly, and then Uncle Keith caught the hungry fish!

I like to go fishing with my dad, and I have even won Boy Scout fishing contests! We have contests for the biggest fish caught and also for the most fish caught. With my dad by my side, I have won both of these contests. I am sure that Uncle Keith is happy that I like to fish, too.

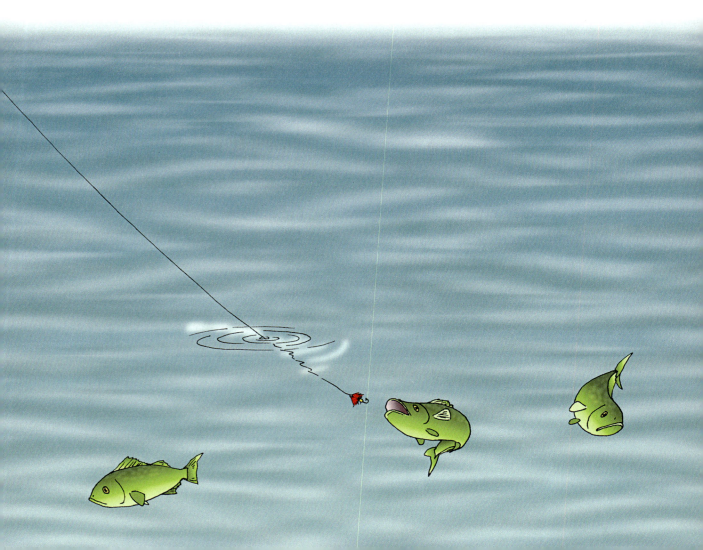

I love hearing stories about Uncle Keith, and my mother always tries to answer my questions. My mom is always a very good listener — maybe that is because she is a clinical social worker. A social worker gives people a safe place to talk about their feelings. If someone is having troubling thoughts, she gives them different ways to feel better. Sometimes when people have tried different ways to feel better, and talking does not seem to be enough, she gives them the phone number of a doctor who can give them medicine to help them feel better. People come to my mother with many different feelings, and she says it is okay to talk about your feelings — whatever they may be, so I knew I could ask her all about Uncle Keith.

I was troubled because I knew Uncle Keith died when he was twenty-nine years old, but I really did not know why he died. So, one day I asked my mother about why he died. "Mom, what caused Uncle Keith to die?"

"Keith died by suicide, or we can say Keith took his own life. Keith was very sick with depression, Cody. Uncle Keith did not want to die, but he felt that his sadness would never end."

"What is depression?"

"Depression is an illness of the brain. When something goes wrong in the brain, the suffering can be very painful. There are certain chemicals in the brain that make people happy and sad. Sometimes the brain doesn't make or mix the chemicals correctly. If this happens, a person's thinking can become confused. We will never know what Uncle Keith was going through before his death. If Keith felt he could live his life as it was before his depression, he would not have wanted to die."

I asked my mom if Uncle Keith knew he was depressed.

"Keith knew he was in a lot of pain, however, he didn't know he was suffering from a treatable illness. Keith's thinking was confused, and he didn't know how he could ever feel happy again. He did not want to admit he needed help with his depression; he thought he could get better by himself."

"Why didn't Keith's family and friends try to help him feel better?"

"Keith wanted to 'be strong' for his family and friends so he hid his feelings from us. Keith always looked like he was happy. It was like he was wearing a mask to hide his feelings of sadness. Keith did not tell anyone that he was suffering with such great pain."

"Why did Uncle Keith hide his feelings of sadness?"

"Maybe Uncle Keith was worried about how people would react to his depression. Some people think that we should snap out of our sad feelings and feel happy again — but you know, Cody — to tell someone to do this would be like telling a person with a broken leg to walk."

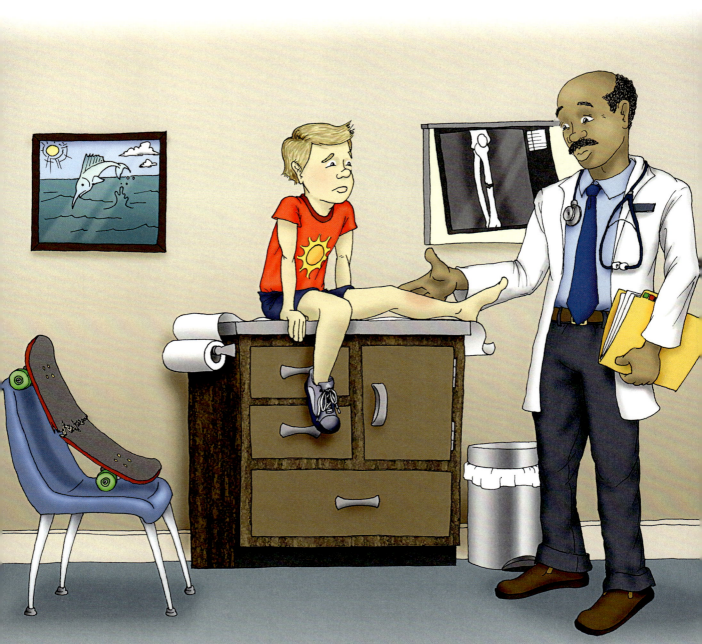

"I sometimes get sad, too, is that depression?"

"Well, all of us get feelings of sadness sometimes — and these feelings are normal — but depression is an illness. It is important to know that being sad or feeling blue is usually not an illness. When a person is sad, he or she usually understands that this sadness will go away with time. Depression, however, can fill people with pain, and they want the pain to stop. They think they will always be depressed and their pain will last forever. They think they will never be happy again, so they feel hopeless."

"You said that depression is an illness, right? Cancer and diabetes are illnesses, but people who have these illnesses tell their families and friends."

"Yes, depression is an illness, Cody, but too many people do not understand that it is an illness. Many people think that depressed people are just sad and that they should find something that would make them happy again. They think: *Snap out of it! Be happy!* Some people even think if depressed people can't be happy, then they are weak. This idea keeps depressed people from going to a doctor to get the medical help they need."

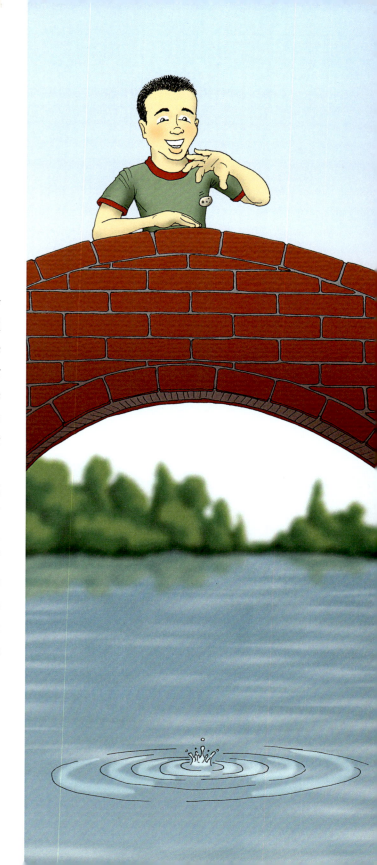

"Mom, what can I do? I know Uncle Keith would want me to tell people that we should never give up, and we need to talk about our feelings — especially when those feelings make us sad. If people do not get the help they need for their depression, people will keep dying."

"Cody, we all can do something to help. I remember my grandmother often told me, 'We only need a small pebble to create a big wave.' Everyone can do something to make a difference in the lives of our friends and family. However, we need to take the first step and pay attention to the feelings of others."

"I try to be a good friend to others and not hurt them or make them feel bad. I listen to them, and I don't make fun of them if they tell me about their feelings. I always try to cheer them up, too."

"Yes, Cody, that is very important, but what if your friend told you that he was very sad and didn't want to be sad anymore? What if this friend stopped playing with you and his other friends and wanted to be alone? What if your friend got angry, stopped doing his homework, and failed his tests in school? Even though you tried to cheer him up, nothing worked. What if your friend wanted you to know about his sadness, but he wanted you to keep it a secret?"

"My friends have told me secrets, and I do keep their secrets — but this is different, right Mom?"

"Yes, it is very different; you need to find help for your friend! This friend really *needs* your help because his thinking is confused; he might be depressed. So, what would you do?"

"I would tell someone about his sadness. I wouldn't tell just anyone though. I wouldn't be able to get him the help he needed. I would only tell someone I trusted like my coach, my teacher, or my counselor at school — and I would tell you, too, Mom!"

"Good for you, Cody, that is what a friend really is! We are not doctors, but we can act out of love. We can stop depression one person at a time."

"Maybe that is why Uncle Keith seems so alive to me, because he knows I can help people understand depression."

"Yes, Cody, that is how *one small pebble can create a wave* — and that one small pebble might be you!"

Picture drawn by Cody Cosentino, July 2006

Discussion Guide
Juli Cosentino, LCSW
Licensed clinical social worker
MA in clinical social work, University of Chicago

How do we tell the children? When suicide devastates the family, many adults struggle to answer that question. Unfortunately, there is no perfect way to talk to children about suicide, and — since many adults feel uncomfortable speaking about this sensitive topic — the first step adults must take is to educate themselves.

Adults often find they are at a loss for words when attempting to talk about suicide, and traditional language related to suicide does not help in this regard. Outdated and inaccurate language contributes greatly to the unwarranted stigma that surrounds suicide. Traditional language implies that the person who died by suicide was somehow responsible for his or her actions, so it is important not to use terms such as "committed suicide" because there should be no shame attached to dying by suicide. Society needs to be aware that those who die by suicide do not actually "make a choice," but die because they lack proper brain chemistry, and that results in severe depression. The despair generated by severe depression leads the brain to think that the only way out is death. Chemical brain disorders cause death by suicide — much the same way that cancer and heart attacks cause death. As society begins to understand this, the stigma of suicide will fade, and adults will become more comfortable talking about suicide to their children as well as other adults.

How did he die? When a child asks this question, an answer is necessary. Never tell your child that you don't want to talk about it or that they are not old enough to understand because this type of response will close the door to open communication. A better answer would be to tell your child that you want to give him/her an answer, but you have to think for a while about how to explain it. Let your child know that as soon as you have thought about your explanation, that you will get back to him/her. It is imperative that your response be prompt; do not let days go by, as the child may think his question is unimportant to you. Your initial response needs to be brief and easily understood. "He died because his brain was sick" is truthful, and this may be all the information your child needs at the time. Let your child lead the conversation — he will let you know if he needs more information.

"What do you mean his brain was sick?" "Why didn't he go to the doctor?" These questions are more complicated; however, they still need to be answered simply and truthfully. Explain to your child that sometimes people's brains don't work the correct way, and when this happens, they feel very sad. Remember: This is a teachable moment — use this opportunity to explain to your child that people should never feel too embarrassed to talk about their feelings. Help your child understand the importance of telling a trusted adult if they ever feel very sad.

"What did his body do to him that he died?" This question will eventually come up, so it is a good idea to have possible responses in mind. Again, a matter-of-fact response is the best choice, and it will not scare a child if you consider your child's developmental level. Again, let the child lead the conversation, and when you feel that the child is ready for more details, just state the facts. Watch how your child reacts to stressful situations in his or her environment. If you feel that your child is not ready for more detailed information, your response should be a preparation for further discussion. Let your communication draw from the child's own life events; i.e., children can be reminded of times they felt so bad that they did things they normally wouldn't do such as breaking something or hitting someone.

Honest, brief, and direct answers will lead you throughout the discussion with your child about difficult topics such as suicide. If you truly feel that you cannot provide your child with the information he or she needs, seek help from your doctor or a qualified child therapist.

Carol Ann (Ilijanich) Loehr graduated from Purdue University with a BA in Elementary and Special Education. She was an elementary and special education teacher.

Her son Keith died by suicide on March 29, 1999. At the time of Keith's death, she had no knowledge of suicide and was inundated with inaccurate, outdated descriptions and "facts" about suicide and its causes. She created and continues to maintain TheGiftofKeith.org, a Web site of information to help comfort and educate survivors of suicide, as well as clergy, health care professionals, and counselors.

Carol serves on the SKIIP's (Super Kid...Informed/Involved Parent) Management Team whose Web site, skiip.org, has current information and Internet resources to understand childhood-onset illnesses of the brain.

She has written many articles: "Not a Matter of Choice," "Suicide: Some Understanding Is Certain to Initiate and Develop Empathy," and "Understanding Keith's Death." These articles have been published in various magazines and newspapers.

Carol works with The Compassionate Friends, a worldwide organization for supporting bereaved families following the death of a child.